OFF
COURSE

OFF COURSE

K. R. COLEMAN

DARBY CREEK

MINNEAPOLIS

Darby Creek
An imprint of Lerner Publishing Group, Inc.
241 First Avenue North
Minneapolis, MN 55401 USA

For reading levels and more information, look up this title at www.lernerbooks.com.

Main body text set in Janson Text LT Std 12/17.5.
Typeface provided by Adobe Systems.

Library of Congress Cataloging-in-Publication Data

Names: Coleman, K. R., author.
Title: Off course / K.R. Coleman.
Description: Minneapolis : Darby Creek, [2020] | Series: [Road trip] | Summary: On an eventful road trip down the Coastal Highway, future video game designer Livi prepares for a college interview and her twin sister, Nora, works on getting into film school.
Identifiers: LCCN 2019006853 (print) | LCCN 2019009215 (ebook) | ISBN 9781541557048 (eb pdf) | ISBN 9781541556881 (lb : alk. paper) | ISBN 9781541573000 (pb : alk. paper)
Subjects: | CYAC: Automobile travel—Fiction. | Sisters—Fiction. | Twins—Fiction. | Motion pictures—Production and direction—Fiction. | College choice—Fiction.
Classification: LCC PZ7.1.C644 (ebook) | LCC PZ7.1.C644 Off 2020 (print) | DDC [Fic]—dc23

LC record available at https://lccn.loc.gov/2019006853

Manufactured in the United States of America
1-46122-43497-6/4/2019

Dedicated to my twin sisters,
Heidi and Heather

CHAPTER
1

Nora stood up through the car's sunroof, a camera in her hand.

"This is a terrible idea!" yelled her sister, Livi, who was driving.

"It's a great idea!" Nora yelled back. She wanted to capture the winding, foggy coastal highway. She pointed her lens and steadied her camera. The sound of the ocean crashing against the black cliffs drifted up from far below.

The fog is perfect, she thought as she filmed.

Her application to a film school in New York required a silent fifteen-minute film. It was due in two weeks. She'd been working on different versions of it for three months, but she didn't like any of them. This road trip with Livi was her last chance to shoot some new scenes.

"Get back inside," Livi yelled from below.

"One more minute," Nora yelled back.

Through the fog, a pair of headlights appeared, accompanied by the deep hum of a distant engine. Nora lifted her camera to capture the approaching vehicle, and as she did the roar grew louder and louder. The headlights were suddenly surrounded by a huge, dark shape. A semi truck. It charged out of the fog. Then, suddenly, it veered over the center line. Livi blasted the horn.

Their car swerved right, nearly hitting the guardrail. Nora braced herself with one hand and held onto her camera with the other. She could smell the truck's diesel fuel. Below, her sister's free hand held tight to her jeans to keep her from flying out of the car.

The semi barreled past them, never stopping or even slowing. In a flash, it disappeared around the foggy bend.

Nora slid back down through the sunroof
and collapsed into her seat. She was surprised
her camera was still in her hand. She was
surprised she was still alive. After settling and
redoing her seatbelt, she held up her camera
and rewound the footage. The shot of the semi
barreling through the fog was incredible.

"I thought you were going to die!" Livi
yelled. Her face was gray, her knuckles white.
"I feel like I'm going to throw up. I need to get
out of this car."

She put on the blinker and began to
pull over.

"We can't stop here," said Nora. The

shoulder was narrow and another car or truck could come through the fog and hit them from behind. "Just keep going. There will be somewhere to turn off soon."

As they approached a bridge, the car's headlights reflected off three white, wooden crosses stuck in the dirt off to the side. They marked a place where a car had crashed. Nora watched as they disappeared behind them.

"That could've been us," said Livi.

"I don't remember this road being so crazy," said Nora. When they had planned this trip, she'd imagined the coastal highway being filled with amazing ocean views. Now she realized it was more dangerous than she remembered. It bent and curved along cliffs that dropped a hundred feet to jagged black rocks below.

The wheels of the car rattled over the bridge. *Thump. Thump. Thump.* The fog seemed to make the entire bridge disappear.

Nora carefully placed her camera back into its black bag.

"Please tell me there's a turn-off soon," said Livi.

Nora took out her phone and looked at a map.

"Hidden Beach is just a mile down the road," she said. "We should pull over and wait for this fog to lift."

They'd waited until noon to leave their campsite to be safe. The fog usually burned off as soon as the sun was high in the sky, but the sun never seemed to come out that morning.

"Actually, it was a mistake to drive in general," Livi said. "I should've just flown down to San Francisco."

Livi had a college interview at Manford University the next day. Nora had convinced her that they should make it a road trip. She wanted the two of them to do something fun together. After all, next year, if they both got into the schools they wanted, they would end up on opposite coasts. It would be the first time in their lives they'd be apart.

They both squinted through the windshield, searching for the turn-off. People often commented on how similar their expressions were. But that was usually after noticing that everything else about their appearances was different. Livi wore her thick, dark hair up in a ponytail that made her look taller. Nora wore her hair short, just to her chin. Recently she had added bright magenta streaks to her hair and gotten a nose ring.

"Mom would kill us if she knew we drove through this," Livi said. She adjusted the rearview mirror that Nora had knocked with her leg.

"If we don't say anything, she'll never know."

They had promised their mother they were responsible enough to make the drive from Portland to San Francisco themselves. Together they'd mapped out their route, marking the places they would stop along the way. They'd decided to break up the twelve-hour drive into two six-hour days.

The night before, they had camped out on a beach. It was exactly the fun adventure Nora had promised her sister. They watched a pod of dolphins play in the ocean. They built a real fire and pitched a tent. Then they stayed up late talking and laughing.

They'd even seen a shooting star race across the sky.

"Okay," Nora had said. "You know what that means. Make a wish."

"Okay," said Livi. "I want to live in the Bay Area and design video games. Maybe even have my own company someday." She shifted in her sleeping bag. "Tell me yours."

"I want to direct my own movies and win an Oscar," Nora had said.

She could see it clearly: her movie's premiere, the opening credits, her name flashing onscreen . . .

Nora snapped out of the memory at the sound of Livi's voice.

"Nora! Is this the turn?" Livi glanced at her, and Nora checked the map again.

"I think that's the sign," said Nora. She glimpsed a small parking lot through the trees. "Yeah, this is it." They pulled in near a blue truck, two other cars, and a black Jeep.

"Do you think people are surfing in this?" asked Livi as they got out. They had both recognized the racks on top of the other cars.

"I hope so," said Nora. She thought it would be great to get a shot of someone surfing through the fog. She was about to tell Livi this, but Livi was looking down at her phone.

"Who are you texting?" she asked.

"Mia," said Livi. "I'm letting her know we'll be late and not to wait up for us. I told her we'd try to get there by six, but now we'll be lucky if we make it by midnight."

Mia had been a year ahead of them in school and now went to Manford herself. She was the one who'd convinced Livi to apply there. Mia and Livi had become close when they designed their own app for the science fair a few years ago.

"Once the fog lifts, we'll make up the time," Nora said. "Especially if I'm driving."

Livi laughed.

"Let's check out the beach," she said, nodding to a steep path.

"First text Mom," said Nora. "Tell her everything is great."

"So, don't mention we almost got run off the road by a semi while one of her daughters was hanging out of the sunroof," said Livi.

"No, don't mention that part." They laughed as Nora grabbed her camera out of the car.

The parking lot was near the top of a cliff, the beach down below. As they headed down the path toward the sound of crashing waves, they breathed in the scent of salt and sea and damp eucalyptus trees. Nora and Livi both loved the ocean. It was why they had decided to travel down the coastal highway instead of taking the interstate through the valley.

Nora zipped up her fleece jacket and shifted her camera bag to her other shoulder.

"Can't you just leave that thing behind?" said Livi.

"Are you kidding?" said Nora. "This thing is my baby. And besides, I need a few more shots. I've decided that this fog is going to be the star of my film."

Livi shook her head. "Something happens when you get behind that camera," she said. "It's like you forget the rest of the world exists."

"The same thing happens when you're on

your computer," said Nora. "You don't even hear me when I'm three feet away."

When they were younger, they had spent hours making movies together. Livi wrote the script and recruited neighbor kids to play different parts. Nora filmed everything with a huge video camera they'd bought at a garage sale for $25. Nora had always imagined them making a real movie together someday, but Livi had lost interest in movies. Now all she thought about was video games and apps and how she was going to make her first million by age twenty-one.

They walked in silence down the dirt path, their hands shoved into their jacket pockets to keep warm.

Down on the beach, the sisters went
their separate ways. Livi searched for shells
and sea glass. Nora walked along the beach,
looking out at the ocean. The waves were
huge. She searched for surfers somewhere
out in the fog.

Halfway down the beach, she caught a
glimpse of a small group of black wetsuits
bobbing in the mist. They appeared and
disappeared like ghosts. She headed to a large,
dark rock that stood near the water's edge and
climbed up onto it to get a better view.

Nora focused the camera on the surfers
and began to film as a large wave took shape

behind them. The wave rolled toward the group. The surfer with a red stripe on his wet suit paddled toward it and disappeared into the fog, only to reappear standing up a second later. He looked as if he were riding on a cloud.

Nora filmed the surfer, the wave unfurling across her screen. It was a beautiful scene, but the wave was growing larger and larger. It reared up over the surfer and crashed down, devouring him in one gulp.

Where did he go? Nora zoomed in on the place where he'd disappeared. She scanned the water with her camera. There was no sign of him or the surfboard.

She moved the camera away from her face and tried to peer through the fog, but all she saw was another wave. It was bigger than the one before. She thought she saw the surfer's bobbing board, but she didn't see him anywhere. The second wave crashed over the surfboard.

"Nora!" yelled Livi. "Watch out!"

Nora looked up and saw a giant wave gain strength and height as it bore down on the beach. It was larger than the rock she was standing on.

Of course, her first concern was for her camera. She zipped it quickly back into its bag.

"Catch," she yelled. Nora threw the bag down to Livi as she leaped off the rock. She fell on her knees into the sand. Before she could stand back up, the giant wave hit her from behind, knocking her flat to the ground. It tried to pull her into the ocean, but she dug her hands and feet into the sand, held her breath, and was able to keep from being pulled into the surf.

The water receded and Nora coughed, gasping and dripping water. Livi grabbed her hand and helped her to stand. She dragged her away from the water before another giant wave came barreling down.

A voice called, "You okay?" One of the surfers was running toward them. He looked to be about their age. He was still in his wet suit and his hair, long and dark, hung in curls around his face.

Nora couldn't speak. She could only

spit out salt water and sand. Livi held onto her shoulder.

"Man, those waves turned into monsters out there," said the surfer. "I just got raked."

Livi pushed Nora's wet hair away from her face so she could peer into her eyes. "Hey," she said. "Are you okay?"

Nora just said, "My camera." She looked past her sister to the black camera bag sitting on the beach. She stood shakily and hurried toward it. Satisfied it was unharmed, she picked up the bag and put it safely back on her shoulder.

"I'm starting to think that camera is jinxed," said Livi as Nora returned. "It's going to end up killing you."

The surfer looked at Nora, who was shivering in her wet clothes. "You know, we've got a fire going down the beach," he said. "Do you want to come warm up? That ocean is cold as ice."

"Colder," said Nora.

"Here, come on." He set off toward the orange glow of a campfire in the distance.

The girls exchanged a glance.

"It's probably fine," Nora said. "He doesn't look like a murderer."

Livi sighed. "Nobody *looks* like a murderer," she said. "But you do look freezing."

They hurried to catch up with the surfer.

"I'm Luca, by the way." He stopped to grab his surfboard out of the sand. Nora and Livi introduced themselves and explained how they'd pulled off the highway because of the fog.

"A semi nearly took us out, and that was the last straw," concluded Livi.

"Must be a storm brewing out there somewhere," said Luca, nodding at the ocean. "Plus there's a full moon tonight. A sailor's moon, as they say."

"Is that what's kicking up those waves?" asked Nora.

Luca nodded. "And those waves kicked my butt."

Nora noticed the red stripe on his wet suit and realized he was the surfer she'd been filming.

"I saw you go down," she said. "You disappeared for a long time. I'm glad you're okay."

"Yeah, that wave was really powerful. Felt like it pushed me down to the bottom." He shivered. "I had to paddle back to shore to catch my breath."

They came to the small fire and gathered around it. Luca's friends' gear lay strewn about. Luca opened up an orange backpack, took out a towel, and gave it to Nora.

"Thanks," she said. She dried her face and hair and wrapped it around her shoulders.

"I'm going to find some more driftwood," said Livi, looking at Nora with concern. She wandered off as Nora sat down on a log and tried to warm up.

* * *

Nora and Luca sat quietly for a while, exchanging small smiles every so often.

"Are you feeling warmer?" Luca asked.

"Slowly but surely," Nora replied.

Luca looked out toward the water. "I can't believe those guys are still out there," he said.

"Speaking of," said Nora. "I think I got a great shot of you surfing. Do you want to see it?"

"Yeah." He moved closer to her as she took out her camera. "You were recording me?" He grinned.

"Filming," Nora corrected.

She carefully took out the camera and examined it.

"That's a sweet camera," said Luca.

"Took me two years to save up for it." Nora turned it on and rewound the footage. "Check out this shot I got of you." She pushed play.

"That's crazy," Luca said, watching himself catch a wave. "I look like I'm floating on a cloud."

Nora smiled. That was exactly the shot she'd wanted.

"And then . . ." said Nora.

They watched the tiny screen as the wave rose up out of the fog and slammed into Luca.

"Man," he said. "The ocean sure is mean today."

"A bully," Nora agreed, returning her camera to its bag. Beaches and cameras, she decided, didn't mix.

"What are you going to do with that footage?" asked Luca.

"I'm applying to film school," said Nora.

"Where?"

"New York. There's an amazing program out there."

Livi returned and threw a few pieces of driftwood onto the fire. "My sister is going to be a famous director someday," she said. "Unless she kills herself filming first." Sparks danced in the air and then floated away, fading.

Suddenly Luca stood. "Speaking of films, wait till you see this," he said. He grabbed his backpack and took out his phone. "My friend Carlos and I were hiking a few days ago and stumbled across a movie set out in the middle of nowhere." Luca scrolled through his pictures. "Check it out." He handed Nora his phone.

"No way!" Nora stopped at a photo of a director sitting high up on a platform behind a camera. "That's Cameron McGregor!" She recognized his red beard and bald head. She wanted to be just like him someday. He'd won a Best Picture Oscar when he was just 26 years old.

"Swipe to the next photo," said Luca.

Nora moved her finger across the phone. There was a photo of a tall, muscular woman with long, dark hair standing near a river and reading through a script.

"Wait," said Nora, zooming in, "That's Rennie Larkin!" She looked at Luca, excited. "There were rumors about a sequel, but no one knew if they were true. Are they finally making the sequel to *The Sacred Place*?"

"I'm pretty sure that's what they were filming," said Luca. "Everyone had white makeup and cloaks and stuff."

"There's no doubt," said Nora, grinning down at the picture. "It looks like she is back from the dead and ready to wreak her revenge."

The Sacred Place was Nora's favorite movie, mainly because of McGregor's filmmaking. He seemed to have an otherworldly sense for which angle or zoom was just right. She'd watched it dozens of times.

"Where are they filming?" asked Nora as she handed his phone back.

"About an hour from here," he said. "Most people don't know about the place. The land used to be owned by some lumber baron, until one day he refused to cut down any more trees and just let everything grow wild. There's this amazing redwood forest, over twenty thousand acres. The Crescent River runs through it."

"I can't believe you got to watch them film," said Nora. "McGregor doesn't let anyone but actors and crew on his set. Didn't he get arrested once for breaking some reporter's camera?"

"No one knew we were watching," said Luca. "We were up on this ridge looking down. We stayed hidden the whole time."

"I wish I could've been there," said Nora.

"You should go," said Luca.

"How do you know they're still there?" asked Livi.

"I don't," said Luca. "We were there three days ago."

"We should stop there," said Nora, looking

at her sister. "McGregor spends days on his scenes. He's been known to camp out and wait for a perfect sunset."

"We don't have time," said Livi.

"We can just drive past," said Nora, pleading. "We don't even have to stop."

"We're already off schedule," said Livi. "How about on the way back?"

Nora sighed. "Okay, I guess."

"Hopefully they'll still be filming," said Luca. "I'll text you the directions."

Nora reached for her phone and felt the empty pocket of her wet jeans.

"My phone," she said, standing up to pat down all her pockets. "It's gone."

"Probably swept out to sea," said Livi.

Nora was too distracted to be upset. "Text me on Livi's," she told Luca. She rattled off her sister's number while Livi sat by, frowning. Luca typed the number into his phone and sent the location of the movie set.

"The text isn't going through," he said after a moment. "There's no cell towers around here. We'll have to do this old school."

He reached into his backpack, took out a notebook and pencil, and drew a map.

Miller's Estate, he wrote. *Five miles off the 101.*

"We should get going," said Livi, standing up and looking at the sky. The fog had begun to lift. The sun was breaking through the gray clouds and patches of blue were peeking out.

"Livi has a college admissions interview tomorrow," Nora explained.

"Where?" asked Luca.

"Manford University," said Livi.

"No way," said Luca. "My friend Carlos had his interview there last week."

"How did it go?" Livi asked.

"He said they asked him some pretty deep questions."

"Like what?"

"I'm not sure," said Luca. "He said he'd tell me more about it later. I could give you his number, if you want."

"That's okay," said Livi. "I have a friend I'm meeting with tonight. She went through the interview a year ago and she told me she'd help me prepare."

Nora unwrapped the towel from her shoulders and handed it back to Luca.

"Thank you," she said. "We should really get going."

"Carlos and I might go and check out the movie set tonight or tomorrow," said Luca. "He's a huge fan too. I'll text you and let you know if they're still filming."

"That would be great," said Nora, flashing him a smile.

He walked with them down the beach and back to the path that led up to the parking lot.

"Good luck with everything," he yelled as they neared the lot.

At the top of the path, Nora turned around. She saw Luca grab his surfboard and head back into the ocean. The map to the movie set was clutched tight in her hand. If they'd had more time, she'd drive there right now.

CHAPTER 4

Back at the car, Nora dug through her duffle bag and pulled out some clean clothes. She regretted not packing another jacket or sweatshirt. All she had were a few T-shirts and an extra pair of jeans. Though the sun was out, she shivered. The clothes she had on were not only wet, but salty and covered in sand.

"Here," said Livi, digging through her bag to pull out a blue cardigan. "Wear this. It will keep you warm."

"Are you sure?" asked Nora. "It's your lucky sweater."

"You're the one who needs some luck right

now," said Livi, looking at her sister. "I can't deal with another close call."

"I think my luck has changed," said Nora. She held up the map that Luca had drawn. He'd written his phone number at the bottom.

"I didn't think you'd be so into a surfer dude," said Livi.

"He wasn't just a surfer dude," said Nora. "He was a really nice guy." She smiled. "I wish I could've talked to him longer."

"You have his number," said Livi. "You can call him."

"*You* have his number," said Nora. "My phone's gone, remember?"

Nora slipped into the backseat of the car and changed into the dry clothes. When she stepped back out, she felt much warmer. She had on Livi's sweater and the sun was shining. She put her hands in her pockets and went to stand next to Livi, who was staring out at the ocean.

"Are you ready?" asked Nora.

"Not really," said Livi. A serious look came over her face. "Maybe we should turn around. Head back home."

"What?"

"I can't shake this bad feeling," said Livi. "I've had it for days. And bad things happen in threes. You're only on number two."

"We aren't turning back," said Nora, looking at her sister. "Admissions is expecting you in the morning. And you've been preparing for this interview all week."

Livi picked up a stone and threw it over the edge of the cliff. "What if I'm not good enough?" she said.

"Come on, Liv," said Nora. "Manford would be lucky to have you."

Livi picked up another rock, held it in her hand, and looked back toward the ocean. "The last few nights, I haven't slept," she confessed. "I've had this dream where I'm in the interview, but I can't answer any of the questions because all my teeth start to fall out. I can feel them piling up on my tongue. It feels so real."

Nora knew her sister was nervous about the interview, but she hadn't realized how nervous.

"Your teeth aren't going to fall out," she told Livi. "You're going to rock this interview.

You're smart. You're focused. And you're a computer-programming beast."

"But what if my words don't come out? What if I sit there and have nothing to say?" Livi chucked the second rock out to the ocean. "I feel like everyone who goes to Manford is way smarter and better than me."

Though she didn't say so, Nora felt the same way about film school. She was afraid of not only being rejected, but of actually getting in and being the worst student there.

"I have an idea," she said, to distract both of them. "You drive and I'll film you answering the questions I ask."

Livi shook her head.

"Come on," said Nora. "It will get you ready for your interview. We'll play it back tonight and figure out what you should do more and what you should do less. It'll be good practice." She offered Livi a smile. "Football players do it all the time. They study their actions and reactions. It makes them better players."

Livi glanced at Nora, then sighed.

"Fine," she said finally. "I'm feeling desperate. I really want to ace this."

"You will," said Nora. "Just be you."

She took out her camera and began to film.

"Maybe you should be me in the interview instead," said Livi hopefully. "You are way calmer under pressure."

Nora laughed. "Remember when we switched classes all the time in second grade?"

"Mrs. Jenson never knew," said Livi, smiling.

"No one could tell us apart back then."

"No, they couldn't."

"Now look at us," said Nora, and she turned the camera and leaned back so she could get a shot of the two of them. "Do you think people would even guess we're twins?"

They both waved at the camera at the same time.

CHAPTER
5

As Livi drove, Nora filmed her answering question after question.

"What literary character do you most admire?"

"Where do you see yourself in ten years?"

"What is your greatest weakness?"

"What is your greatest strength?"

An hour down the road, Livi was answering the questions more naturally. The words rolled off her tongue. She seemed to get her confidence back. Nora set the camera down, reached into a cooler in the backseat, and took out two sodas to celebrate.

"You've got this," she said, and they clinked

their aluminum cans together.

Nora cranked up some music and Livi rolled the windows down. The fog was gone. The road was clear. They were making good time again.

Nora picked up her camera and filmed Livi's hair blowing in the breeze. Livi looked relaxed and happy. This was how Nora hoped her sister would come across in the interview.

A few miles down the road, Nora saw hills covered in orange poppies.

"Livi?" Nora began hopefully, turning the music down.

Livi cut a glance at her. "You want to stop, don't you?"

"The hills look like a scene from *The Wizard of Oz*." Nora looked out the window. They'd always watched *The Wizard of Oz* together. One Halloween they even both dressed up as Dorothy.

"But weren't the poppies a trap?" said Livi.

"Five minutes," said Nora. "Just a quick shot. I want to film the flowers with the ocean in the background." She looked back at her sister. "Please? What can go wrong in a field of flowers?"

"Fine," said Livi. "But we're stopping and you're getting out of the car. I'm not letting you stick your head out the sunroof again."

"Deal," said Nora. Livi put on the blinker and took a left turn onto a gravel road.

Nora grabbed her camera and ran to the top of the hill. She filmed the bright orange flowers swaying against the blue sky. Knowing Livi wanted to get back on the road, she tried to be quick with her shots.

As Nora headed down the hill and back to the car, she saw Livi picking a bouquet of wild flowers. She stopped to film her sister. The wind ruffled Livi's hair and the sun brightened her cheeks. Nora zoomed in on Livi's face, trying to catch her expression. As Nora filmed, a small black dot rose next to her sister's ear.

"Liv, I think there's a bug by you," Nora said. A second dot rose, then a third.

Nora watched through her camera lens as Livi turned, noticed the bees, and screamed.

A swarm of bees rose up from the ground,

buzzing angrily. In a flash, they flew at Livi, surrounding her. She flailed her arms at them and began to run, but tripped and fell to the ground. Nora ran to help her sister.

"Get them off!" Livi screamed as bees swarmed her face.

Nora grabbed Livi's arm and the two sisters ran to the car as the bees attacked. Nora swatted at the bees, but they lunged and stung her arms and hands. Stabbing pains shot over her skin.

When they reached the car, Nora opened the back door and shoved Livi inside. "Oh, it hurts," Livi groaned, covering her face with her hands.

Nora slammed the door shut, but not before a handful of bees followed them in.

"Kill them," Livi said as the bees angrily buzzed.

Nora took off her shoe and smashed two against the window. She killed one against the seat and then one against her own neck as it stung her.

Livi took her hands away from her face.

One of her eyes was red and swollen. Nora counted four giant welts. They seemed to grow redder and more inflamed every second, as if Livi were having a reaction. "Wait, you're not allergic, are you?" Nora asked, panicking. "Can you breathe?"

Livi nodded. "But my face feels like it's on fire," she whimpered.

"Hand me the keys and your phone."

Nora searched on Livi's phone for the nearest medical clinic. The internet was slow and shaky, fading in and out. Finally a red dot appeared on the map, but the clinic was thirty miles away. Then she remembered the first-aid kit their mother had made them bring. It was in the trunk of the car.

The swarm of angry bees was still buzzing outside the window.

"Hold on," said Nora. She climbed into the front seat and started the car. She drove until they were clear of the bees, then pulled over, popped the trunk, and grabbed the first-aid kit.

Nora opened the back car door and knelt in front of her sister.

"I need to get the stingers out," she said.

Livi closed her eyes. One by one Nora found the tiny black stingers and pulled them out, swabbing each of the bites with antiseptic as she finished. "Now we need to get you some ice."

All the ice in their cooler had melted, but she'd seen a sign for a gas station when they turned off the highway. Nora got back in the car and put it in drive. The back tires kicked up rocks and dust as she sped down the gravel road.

CHAPTER
6

A few miles down the road, Nora spotted
an old gas station sitting at the edge of field.
It looked like a scene from an old movie.
The white paint had faded and peeled, and a
wooden porch sagged in the front.

Nora pulled into the empty parking lot.
She wasn't even sure the place was open. Taped
to each gas pump was a handwritten sign that
said: *Out of Order.*

One window of the store was boarded
up. The other was so covered in dust and
dirt she wondered if the place had been
abandoned years ago. Then she saw a shadow
move behind the grime. She knew whoever

was inside was watching them.

"I'll be right back," said Nora. She grabbed her wallet out of her backpack and slid it into her sweater pocket.

"Maybe I should go with you," said Livi, eyeing the store with her one good eye.

"Let me see if it's even open."

Nora got out of the car. Slowly, she approached the steps leading to the slanted and weather-beaten porch. A sign on the door said it was open, but inside everything looked dark.

Nora pushed the peeling white door and stepped inside.

"Afternoon," a raspy voice said.

Nora's eyes, still adjusting from the sunshine, couldn't make out the man's face. She only saw his bent-over silhouette lurking near the counter.

"Do you have any ice?" she asked, looking around.

The man shuffled to a rusty white freezer and pointed.

Nora took a step toward it. He didn't move.

She was afraid if she opened it herself and bent to pull out a bag of ice, he might push her in and close the lid, and she'd be found by a detective years from now.

"Could you grab a bag for me?" She decided to keep her distance, and kept one eye fixed on the door.

The man opened the lid. It creaked as if it hadn't been opened in years. He pulled out a bag of ice that seemed to have melted and then frozen again. He shuffled to the counter with the bag without saying a word.

"How much?" asked Nora.

"How much do you want to pay?" said the man, grinning.

Nora said, "A dollar?"

"Sounds about right," he said.

Nora noticed some dusty boxes of medicine on a crooked shelf behind the counter. She remembered taking allergy medicine the last time she had been stung. With the ice, it had helped keep the swelling down.

"How much for a box of allergy medicine?" asked Nora, nodding to the shelf.

"You got allergies?" he said, and looked her in the eye.

"No," she said. "My sister and I ran into some bees."

She held out her hand so he could see the welts.

"We've got some Africanized honeybees around here," he said. "Deadly things. Killed a farmer up the road."

"What?" said Nora. She looked out the dirty window, trying to see her sister in the car.

"He got stung over a hundred times. Throat swelled up. Died out in his field. Buzzards circled him. That's how they found him."

Nora pointed to the medicine again.

"I really need to get going," she said.

"How about some candy?" said the man.

She grabbed a candy bar from a wire bin and slapped it on the counter. The man nodded. Then, slowly, he picked up the box of medicine. He said, "How much do you want to pay for this?"

Nora wished she could grab the box from

his hand and run, but he was holding it just out of reach.

"How much is it?" She was sick of this guessing game. "Isn't there a price tag on it?"

"No price tag," said the man. "I like to see what people are willing to offer." He let out a laugh, like this was all a joke to him.

"Twenty dollars for everything." She took out a twenty-dollar bill and placed it on the counter next to the melting bag of ice and the candy bar.

He stared at the money without picking it up.

"Had some fancy Hollywood folk in here a week ago," he said after a moment. "They wanted to shoot a scene in my store. I asked them how much." He looked up at her, grinning again. "You know what they said?"

Nora looked at him and then out at the window at her sister.

"I don't know," she said.

"Guess," he said.

She played along, hoping it would speed up her escape.

"A million dollars?"

"Ten thousand," he said, the grin still on his face. "But it wasn't the money I wanted."

Nora picked up the ice and the candy bar.

"What did you want?" she said, starting to back away.

"A part in the movie they were making," he said. He looked excited about this. "That's what I wanted. To be on the big screen!"

"Do you know where they are now?" she asked.

He set the box of medicine on the counter, took the twenty-dollar bill, and pushed some keys on the old register. "No," he said.

She tried again. "Who were they?"

He took some change out from the register and set it on the counter. Nora reached for the dollar bills. He clapped his cold, bony hand over hers, and she flinched.

"I've been sworn to secrecy," he said. "Signed a contract, even. They don't want anyone knowing about this movie."

"I won't say anything," said Nora, yanking her hand away without the money.

"Your change," he said as she backed away.

She said, "Keep it."

He came from behind the counter.

"Take it," he said, following her across the store.

Nora was afraid that he'd grab her if she didn't. She turned around and took the money from his hand.

He ran his fingers across the few greasy strands of hair on top of his head. He gave a huge smile that revealed two pointy canine teeth.

"I can't say a word about the movie," he said. "But ask me if I got the part."

"Did you?" she asked, still moving toward the door.

He nodded.

Nora turned and bolted out the door.

CHAPTER
7

Livi was standing outside the car. Her face looked worse. Her eye was completely swollen shut and her upper lip looked like she'd been punched. *Bee stung*, Nora wanted to joke, but didn't dare. Livi looked like she was in too much pain.

"What happened to you?" asked Livi. "I was about to go inside and find you."

"I'm glad you didn't go in there," said Nora. She smashed the bag of ice on the ground to break the block of ice up into chunks. "It's a scary place."

She popped open the trunk, took a clean T-shirt from her bag, and filled it with ice so that Livi could hold it to her face.

"I met a creepy, creepy guy," said Nora, nodding to the store. She noticed the man had wiped away the dust on the window to stare at them. "Let's get out of here." They slid back into the car and Nora started the engine. She wanted to be prepared in case the storekeeper came out.

"Ow," said Livi, holding the ice against her eye. She peered at Nora. "You should get your camera and film me. I look like a monster right now—no make-up artist required."

"Keep the ice on your eye," said Nora. She took the box of medicine from her sweater pocket. "This will help too." She opened the box to inspect it. Luckily, the bottle inside looked fine. "Mom gave me this when I got stung by that hornet last summer. It helped take the swelling down."

Livi took a big swig of the medicine straight from the bottle.

"Thank you," she said, leaning back in her car seat. She gently held the bundle of ice against her eye and then took another sip of medicine.

"Maybe we should head to a doctor," said Nora.

"We aren't going to find one around here," said Livi. "Mia will know where to go once we get to the city. Just drive. I'm sure I'll be better in a few hours."

As Nora drove out of the parking lot, she saw the store clerk standing on the porch watching them pull away. She wanted to tell Livi about the part he'd gotten in a movie just a few days ago—a movie she was convinced was the sequel to *The Sacred Place*—but she knew Livi wouldn't want to hear it. Her sister's eyes were closed in pain.

Nora drove slowly and carefully down the road.

When they reached the poppy-covered hill, Nora looked over at Livi. Her welts seemed to have calmed a bit. Nora put the car in park and helped Livi put more ice into the T-shirt.

"How are you feeling?" she asked.

"Like I was stung by an angry mob of bees," said Livi. "But the burning has stopped."

"Good," said Nora

Livi handed her the phone.

"Text Mom," she said. "Tell her we're almost there."

Nora sent off the text. The truth was they were still three hours away.

"Now," said Livi. "Call Manford University and cancel my interview. I can't go looking like this."

"I'm sure the swelling will go down," said Nora.

"And if it doesn't?" said Livi.

"Then you tell them you were attacked by killer bees," said Nora. "I'm sure they'll be impressed that you showed up. And they'll never forget your face."

Livi tried to smile, but couldn't.

"Ow," she said instead.

Nora snapped a picture.

Livi groaned. "Why would you do that?"

"Someday we'll laugh about this," said Nora.

"Someday," said Livi. "But not today."

A text message appeared on the phone. Nora expected it to be from their mom, but it was from Luca.

Carlos heard they're filming tonight. A full moon, it read. *Take Sequoia Road. Location off an unmarked lumber road. We are going to park our car there and hike down to the river.*

"Was that Mom?" asked Livi.

"Yeah," Nora lied. "She said to make sure you get some sleep before your interview."

"Man, I do feel sleepy," said Livi. She leaned her seat back and put the bundle of ice over her eyes.

"It's the allergy medicine," said Nora. "It causes drowsiness. Maybe you shouldn't have taken so much."

"Maybe," Livi mumbled.

Nora pulled up a map on Livi's phone. She looked for Sequoia Road. It cut through a state forest and joined up with another road called Mountain Pass. That road led back to the interstate. Nora thought it might even be a shortcut.

She sat there debating with herself. The interstate was faster than the coastal road, but they would drive away from the ocean. No blue water peeking through the trees. No random beach stops. No roadside fruit stands. Those were the things she had promised Livi—not a flat, crowded, boring interstate. Then again, the situation had changed with the bee attack. And wouldn't Livi want to get to Manford sooner rather than later?

Nora turned to Livi to tell her about the shortcut, but she had fallen asleep.

Let her sleep, Nora reasoned. She turned back onto the coastal highway and headed toward Sequoia Road.

Five minutes, she thought to herself. *No more than ten.*

CHAPTER
8

The turn was coming up fast. Nora saw giant trees rise up along the right side of the road, and on her left, the sun disappearing into the ocean. She began to second-guess driving through the woods and over the small mountain range in the dark.

Stick to the coast, she thought, but then she spotted a white cardboard sign marked with a black arrow. She knew film crews used these signs to mark their location. Sure enough, there was the turn-off for Sequoia Road.

Their mother had taken them to a shoot once, back when they lived in LA. She used to be an actress. The biggest break she ever got was a small part on a sitcom. When that show went off the air after seven years, she gave up acting and moved the three of them to Portland to start a new life. But something about being on the set had stayed with Nora forever.

They're definitely shooting tonight. Nora slowed the car and made a careful turn onto the tree-lined road. She looked down at the map on Livi's phone. No other roads were marked.

Livi shifted in her seat, but didn't wake up.

One mile. Two miles. Three. Nora drove down the road. It grew darker, darker, and harder to see. She looked for another cardboard sign, but saw nothing but giant redwood trees and swaying green ferns.

Finally, she came across an unmarked asphalt road and turned onto it. It led deeper and deeper into the forest. She drove for a while, looking for any signs of a movie set, but there were none. In front of her, the road split into two. Luca hadn't mentioned a fork. She decided to take the road on the right because it looked to be in better shape. But a mile down the road she knew she was wrong. The road was growing narrower and narrower as it curved and climbed upward.

She flicked on her high beams. She didn't know what she'd do if another car or truck came barreling toward them. To the right of the road was a steep drop-off. To the left, boulders and pine trees lined the mountainside. The road grew bumpy. It looked as if a heavy rain had washed away parts of it. She couldn't imagine trucks filled with cameras and props passing through here.

The wheels of the car jolted over a rut.

I need to turn back, thought Nora, but there was no room to turn around. *What if a car comes?*

"Where are we?" said Livi, suddenly sitting up.

"Taking a shortcut," Nora answered calmly, though she was starting to panic. She looked at their fuel gauge and realized they barely had a fourth of a tank left. "I thought I'd cut over to the interstate."

Livi looked out her window into the darkness.

"Seriously," she said. "Where are we?"

But before Nora could answer, Livi yelled, "Watch out!"

A large, dark creature bolted across the road. Nora swerved and slammed on the brakes. The car fishtailed.

"Hold on!" Nora yelled. She gripped the steering wheel and pushed with all her might against the brake, hoping to stop the car from plunging over the edge of the road. The car slowed, but she felt them leave the asphalt. Their wheels thumped and bumped over rocks and debris. The car started rolling down the steep slope.

"Nora!" Livi screamed. A terrible, grating jolt ran through the car: they'd hit a large pine tree in the dark. The front of the car crunched inward as, in slow motion, they came to a stop.

Their headlights shone down into the darkness, and the scene came into view. The lone pine tree was the only thing keeping them from rolling down the steep slope and into a raging river below.

Nora and Livi stared out the windshield. Their airbags hadn't gone off, but the front of their car was completely crushed.

"Are you okay?" asked Nora, her voice shaking. She looked over at her sister.

"No," said Livi. She grabbed the phone and dialed 911.

The tree gave a sudden crack.

"Get out. Now!" Livi yelled, but Nora couldn't open her door. The crushed front had jammed it shut.

Livi tried her door. It flew open and the car shuddered.

"Go!" shouted Nora. Livi climbed out of the car, falling to her hands and knees to keep from sliding down the incline.

Nora climbed into the passenger seat and out the door. She started to slide down the hill too, but grabbed hold of the roots of a scrub brush. "Climb," said Livi.

They started to make their way back up to the road. Suddenly Nora shouted, "Wait! My camera!"

"Are you serious?" Livi yelled. "Just leave it!"

"I can't!" Nora yelled, looking back at the car. "It has all my footage. I haven't backed it up." She began to slide back down the hill.

"No!" Livi screamed. "Nora, stop!"

Ignoring her, Nora made her way to the car. She grabbed onto the back bumper and worked her way to the door. Her camera was in its black bag in the backseat. She couldn't reach it unless she climbed back into the car.

"Nora!" Livi screamed. "Please don't!"

Nora looked up at her sister and then back at her camera.

The tree gave a shudder and a loud cracking sound echoed through the valley. The car lurched forward. Nora leaped out of the car, falling to the ground and scrambling for a handhold. Clinging to a boulder, she watched as the pine tree shuddered again. Its roots moved from the soil and the trunk skewed sideways. The car, loose from its hold, began to roll again. It picked up speed, down the slope and into the river, meeting the water with a splash and gurgle. The headlights glowed for a moment, then flickered and went dark.

"**N**ora!" Livi screamed.

Nora couldn't answer. She was in shock, still clinging to the hillside. She felt her arms grow weak. She almost let go of the boulder.

"Nora!" Livi screamed again. Nora could hear her sister sliding back down the hill.

"I'm okay," said Nora shakily. "Livi, stop. Don't come back down. I'm okay."

Nora turned and managed to climb back up the hill, though she didn't feel okay at all. She felt weak and sick. At the top, Livi reached out her hand and Nora grabbed hold. Together, they stepped back up to the road.

They stood there for a moment, looking down to where their car had disappeared into the darkness. They could hear the river. Nora imagined water spilling into the car. She imagined her camera bag floating in the back seat, the water slowly submerging it, the camera and all her footage destroyed.

Livi took out her phone. It gave off a blue glow as she dialed 911.

After a moment, the phone beeped. "No signal," she said. She held the phone over her head and tried again. "Where are we?" she demanded, turning to Nora.

"Miller's Estate," said Nora. "I think that's the Crescent River down there, but I'm not sure. I might have accidentally veered into a state forest."

"What road did you turn on?" Livi's voice was scarily even.

"I'm not sure," said Nora. "It wasn't marked."

Livi tried calling 911 a third time. Again, the call failed. They both looked at the phone.

"I need to wait to make another call," said Livi. "There's only ten percent battery left."

Livi's voice sounded more scared than Nora had ever heard it.

"We need to move higher up and out of all this tree cover," said Nora.

"How deep into the forest are we?" asked Livi.

"I don't know," said Nora.

"Guess," Livi snapped. "How far did you drive down this road?"

"There was another road before this one," said Nora. "We might be twenty or thirty miles from the coast."

Livi was silent. They started walking uphill to try to get a better signal. A mile or so later they stopped.

"Try calling again," said Nora.

"You try," said Livi, her voice sharp but also tight, as if she might cry. She handed Nora the phone. Nora dialed 911, but the call didn't go through.

Maybe a text will work, she thought. She sent a message to Luca.

Help! Tried to find movie set. Had a car accident. Don't know where we are.

Maybe if he got the message he'd be able to find them. He'd been in this area before. For a moment, it looked as if the message would go through. But then the word *Failed!* appeared in red.

Failed. That's how Nora felt standing there with the phone in her hand. She'd destroyed their car. She'd lost her camera. And worst of all, she'd failed her sister. How was Livi going to get to her interview? How were they going to survive a night in the woods? The air temperature had dropped. It felt just above freezing. Their sleeping bags, their clothes, and their food were all in the car, floating in river water.

"I'm sorry," said Nora, looking at Livi. "I was just going to cut down this road and get to the interstate. I was thinking—"

"You weren't thinking!" Livi yelled. "At least about anyone but yourself! You decided to look for the movie set, didn't you?"

Nora didn't answer.

"I knew it!" Livi snapped. "You decided that was more important than getting us safely to San Francisco. I never should have trusted you to take the wheel!"

"I thought this would be on the way," said Nora lamely.

"This isn't on the way to anything!" Livi shrieked. "We're in the middle of nowhere!"

Livi started walking, saying nothing else. She walked, careful to keep one step ahead of her sister.

The silence hurt Nora worse than the yelling.

"I'm sorry," Nora said again. She didn't know what else to say.

Livi ignored her.

Another mile up the road, they stopped and Nora dialed 911 again. They held their breath and waited for the sound of ringing, but instead they heard a snap. They both felt something lurking above them and looked up into a tree branch hanging over the road.

"What was that?" Livi whispered.

"I don't know," said Nora. She shone the phone's light up into the branches above them. They saw nothing, but still felt the lurking presence. Another twig snapped nearby.

"Nora," Livi hissed. "What if it's a mountain lion?"

"Don't run," Nora warned. "If it is, it'll pounce." They stopped to listen. "I think we're supposed to stand still and make ourselves look bigger," she added.

They put their arms up in the air and waved them around. Everything was quiet.

"Or maybe that was for a bear," said Nora. The two of them backed slowly down the road.

"Can you hear that?" said Livi.

"No," said Nora.

"It sounds like growling!"

Nora had an idea. She put the phone on camera mode.

"What are you doing?" said Livi. "This is no time for pictures! We're about to get eaten!"

Nora pointed the camera at the tree. A flash seared through the darkness. Quiet again.

"Do it again," Livi whispered.

Nora took another picture. The flash went off, and they heard another snap, this time farther away.

Nora snapped a final picture. The rustling was distant now. The phone went dark in her hand.

Nora slipped the dead phone into her pocket and picked up a large stick from the side of the road. Livi picked up a handful of rocks and put them in her sweatshirt pocket. Then she picked up two larger rocks and cracked them together.

"Scat, cat!" Nora yelled as Livi threw a rock into the forest. They listened: nothing.

"Now what?" said Livi.

"We keep moving," said Nora. "We have to get to a main road where we can flag down a car."

They started walking. Livi's stomach growled. They hadn't eaten anything since lunch. Nora felt in the pocket of the sweater and took out the candy bar she'd bought at the creepy store. She handed it to Livi.

Livi unwrapped it, broke it two, and gave Nora the other half. They walked, savoring each bite.

The moon was rising above the trees. There was an aura around it, pink, blue, and yellow.

A sailor's moon, Nora thought to herself.

"What time is it?" asked Livi.

Nora went to grab the phone until she remembered it was dead.

"Close to midnight?" Nora guessed, looking up at the moon.

Livi's stomach growled again. She stopped walking and looked at Nora. "I just want to lie down on this road and sleep for a bit," she said.

"We aren't stopping or sleeping as long as there are mountain lions around," said Nora.

"We have to keep going. The main road can't be that much farther."

They both squinted into the forest.

"What's that?" said Livi, pointing.

Nora looked through the trees, following Livi's finger.

"There's a light," said Nora.

"I see it too."

But the light wasn't coming from the road. It was coming from deep in the woods.

"It could be Miller's Estate," said Livi. "Luca said this was all private land. Maybe there's a house down there."

Nora was quiet, thinking.

"I say we head toward it," Livi added.

Nora didn't answer. She thought she heard something coming down the road.

"I don't know," Nora said finally. "Maybe we should stick to the road."

"That light looks like it's less than a mile away," said Livi. "Come on, Nora. It might even be your movie set."

Nora looked at the light. Livi was right.

"Fine," she said.

The two of them stepped off the road and into the woods. They stumbled across a trail. Nora thought it might be another old logging road. It led downward, deeper and deeper into the forest. Leaves crunched beneath their feet. They jumped every time a stick broke, thinking something was just behind them.

"Stop," said Nora. She heard the sounds of an engine and wheels crunching on gravel. It was coming from the road behind them, growing louder and louder. "A car!" she yelled. "Go, go, go!"

They turned to run back up the trail, but the car was gone by the time they reached the road again. All they could see were the red taillights disappearing over a hill.

"Help!" Nora and Livi both yelled. "Help!" But their voices were lost in the distance. After a moment, they both turned and headed back down the trail.

"We should've stayed on the road," said Nora.

"*You* should've stayed on the road," Livi replied sharply.

"Just watch for the light," said Nora. "I'm sure we'll see it again."

"And if we don't?"

"I don't know," said Nora. "I guess we follow the river. A river always leads to people, right? If we follow it, we'll find someone to help us." Nora met Livi's eyes. "Promise."

Livi groaned. "No more promises you can't keep."

CHAPTER
11

They walked and the trail grew steeper. They found the light again, but it wasn't steady: it seemed to go out for minutes at a time. The trail was covered in sticks and debris, and they stumbled often. They were going deeper and deeper into a valley.

Eventually they began to hear rushing water again. A river—the same one their car was in.

The trail stopped at the river's edge. It looked as if there had once been a wooden bridge, but the planks had washed away. They needed to cross. The light was coming from the other side.

Nora spotted a fallen tree downstream.

"We can cross over that," she said.

They walked down to the tree. It would be tricky to cross over. They'd have to step over knots and branches. Nora climbed onto the trunk and began to cross first.

"Whatever you do, don't fall in," Livi warned. She grabbed onto a branch and walked as if she were on a balance beam behind Nora.

Step by small step they shuffled across the fallen tree, moving slowly and carefully.

Halfway across, Livi stopped. "Do you see that?" she asked.

Nora turned and looked in the direction of her sister, but felt herself starting to wobble. She grabbed hold of a branch and steadied herself. Down the river, through the trees, they could see shadows moving in the light.

Suddenly, a scream echoed deep in the woods. It was a piercing scream, a human scream, like someone was in great pain.

"What was that?" said Nora.

The light suddenly went out, and the two sisters froze.

"We should turn back," Livi whispered.

Nora leaned against the branch and peered through the darkness. As she leaned, her left foot slipped. The branch snapped under her weight, and she was falling. She gasped as she hit the ice-cold water.

"Nora!" Livi screamed.

CHAPTER
12

Nora fought to keep her head above the fast-moving water. She could see a bend in the river up ahead, and there, another fallen tree. Nora willed her numb arms and hands to reach out. Kicking and struggling to keep her head up, she grabbed hold of the wet, slippery tree trunk.

"Nora!" she heard Livi yell.

"Here!" Nora yelled back. "I'm here."

She watched Livi scurry down the riverbank and step into the cold water.

"No!" Nora yelled. "Don't! It's too cold!"

Her sister didn't listen. She waded in deeper and stretched out her arm.

"Grab my hand," Livi yelled. But Nora was afraid that if she let go of the tree, she'd be swept away again.

Livi grabbed onto the tree herself and waded in even further. She found the arm of the sweater Nora was wearing and pulled with all her strength. She was able to pull Nora toward the sandy bank, where they both collapsed, gasping.

Livi grabbed Nora's arm and shook her. "Nora, are you okay?"

Nora couldn't answer. Her teeth were chattering. She saw that Livi was dripping wet too. They crawled further up the riverbank and sat there, shivering.

Nora had no idea what they would do. Most likely, they would freeze to death. They had no dry clothes and nothing to build a fire. She knew they didn't have much time. Her body was shaking and her feet and fingers were numb.

"We need to keep moving," said Livi, and she stood with some effort. Nora looked up at her from the ground. The idea of standing was more than she could bear.

"Liv, I'm exhausted," said Nora. "And we can't get any more lost. We almost just died. Let's wait for a second."

"We can't," said Livi. "We have to find help."

Nora wanted to cry, but she stood. They began to walk, arm in arm. Nora was sure Livi could feel her shaking.

Suddenly the light reappeared. They were on the right side of the river this time. "There," Livi said. They made their way toward the light. It was shining into some sort of clearing. As they got closer, Nora could hear voices.

Out of nowhere, something grabbed her shoulder.

Nora whipped around and saw the man from the store grinning at her.

She screamed.

* * *

Somewhere above them, someone was shouting.

"Cut! Who's screaming? No one should be screaming! I asked for silence on the set!"

All at once, the clearing filled with light. There were cameras everywhere.

Nora looked around in disbelief. She was standing in the middle of a movie set. There were cables running across the ground like black snakes. As she watched, actors appeared from behind the trees. They all had white makeup on their faces and sharp, long fangs—vampires, all of them. This was it. The world of *The Sacred Place*.

She looked at the store clerk. "You really are in the movie," she said weakly.

He grinned and nodded.

"We need help," said Livi. "My sister fell in the river."

Nora watched the man who'd been shouting climb down some scaffolding between two trees. He looked angry. He threw a script on the ground as he marched toward them. Up close, he was unmistakable. It was Cameron McGregor himself, bald head, red beard, and all.

"Who are you?" he demanded, approaching them. "What are you doing on my set?"

Nora was starstruck and couldn't speak.

"My sister fell in the river and she needs to get warm," insisted Livi.

McGregor didn't answer. He just stared them down.

A tall woman wearing a long white dress appeared. Her dark hair hung down to her shoulders. Nora recognized her: it was Rennie Larkin, star of *The Sacred Place*. Instead of white face makeup, she sported a line of fake blood dripping down her neck.

"Oh, my goodness. You two look awful," said Rennie. She looked around for a crewmember. "They need to get warm. Now!" She walked off, yelling for someone to get some blankets.

McGregor looked at Nora.

"Why are you two here?" he demanded. "Who are you working for?"

A young woman—not much older than them—appeared with blankets in her arms. She handed one to Nora and one to Livi.

"We aren't working for anyone," said Livi, wrapping both blankets around Nora.

Rennie reappeared. "Ignore him. Follow me," she said. "We need to get you two warm and dry." She began to lead them to a tent a ways off from the clearing.

"Hey! We have a movie to finish!" McGregor yelled after them.

They reached the tent and Rennie lifted the flap, waving them inside. "Come in," she said. "Let's find you some warm clothes."

The young woman from before arrived with a pile of clothes in her arms. She directed them to the back of the tent, where a modesty curtain divided the space. Nora and Livi stepped behind the curtain, took off their wet, dirty clothes, and slipped into the dry sweatshirts and jeans.

The young woman handed them each a cup of hot coffee when they came out. Nora thought black, bitter coffee had never tasted so good. Another crewmember brought over a plate filled with pastries. Eating and drinking, they settled into some folding chairs inside the tent.

"Thank you so much," Nora said to the young woman. "I'm finally starting to feel my legs again."

"I'm Sadie," the woman said. "I'm Rennie's assistant. When you two are warm and fed,

I can drive you to the local sheriff's station. There's no cell reception around here because of the cliffs."

"Thank you," said Nora, feeling bittersweet. She was still chilled to the bone and her head was swimming. They had to call their mom. She had to explain what had happened to the car, why she'd driven them so far off course, and why Livi hadn't made it to her interview. *Oh*, she thought, heart sinking. Livi's interview.

Nora looked over at Livi, who seemed surprisingly at peace. "Do you think Mia is worried about us?" she asked.

Livi shrugged. "No way to know."

"Maybe we can still get you to Manford on time," said Nora.

"It's funny," Livi said sarcastically. "Since we crashed, I haven't really been worried about that."

Sadie brought over more warm towels. "You two are lucky we're still here," she said. "We were supposed to wrap things up last night, but McGregor wasn't happy with the shots."

"Yeah, I don't think we would've made it much longer," said Livi, and reached for Nora's hand. Nora could feel the warmth of her sister's hand spread to her own.

CHAPTER
13

The tent flap suddenly flew open and McGregor marched in.

"You never answered me," he snapped. "Who are you and what are you doing on my set?"

"Like we told you, we had a car accident," said Livi, standing up from her chair.

"An accident?" snapped McGregor. "I don't think this was any accident. In fact, it looks like someone paid you to find this set and leak the ending to my film."

Nora began, "No! I mean, I did want to see you film—"

"So you were spying?" McGregor cut in. "Just admit it. You're paparazzi." He scowled at the word. "Which tabloid sent you? Where's your camera?"

"My camera?" said Nora, feeling sick. "My camera is in our car in a river."

"So you do have a camera!" said McGregor.

"Enough, Cameron," said Rennie, facing him. "Stop harassing them. They really needed help. They aren't out to get you."

Nora looked McGregor in the eye. "I came here because I'm a fan of yours," she said. "I came because your movies made me want to go to film school. I have a camera in my car because I was working on a film of my own. Livi and I are just high school students. We were on our way to San Francisco for my sister's college interview until I messed everything up."

McGregor stared at Nora. Rennie cut in. "These two have clearly been through a lot," she said. "They just need to rest and they'll be on their way. We have a movie to finish, so let's stay focused on what needs to be done."

McGregor was still scowling, but he turned away and exited the tent. They heard him yell,

"Everyone, back in your places. We're running out of time, and the moonlight is perfect. We need two more scenes to wrap this up and if we don't get them, we'll have to wait another month to shoot again."

Rennie looked at Nora and Livi. "Are you two going to be okay?" she asked.

"We're fine," said Nora. "Please, go finish your scenes. I've waited forever for this sequel."

"She's watched *The Sacred Place* a hundred times," said Livi. "She knows every line."

"In that case," said Rennie. "If you two feel up to it, come out and watch us film a few scenes."

Nora's eyes went wide.

Rennie smiled and turned to Sadie. "Show them where they can sit."

* * *

Sadie led Livi and Nora to a different pair of folding chairs on set. They sat down next to each other, matching in their sweatshirts and jeans.

"You two are identical," said Sadie, looking

them up and down. "I didn't notice at first that you were twins, but now I do."

"Womb-mates," said Nora, linking her arm through Livi's.

"I have a womb-mate too," said Sadie.

"Really?" said Nora.

"I have a brother," said Sadie. "We're totally different, but totally the same. Womb-mate . . ." She paused, smiling a little. "I love that. I can't wait to tell Charlie that phrase."

"Two minutes!" someone yelled. "Take your places."

Actors disappeared into the woods. They watched Rennie go to her place, a boulder in the middle of a small creek. A crewmember came to arrange her dress.

"It needs more mud and rips," Rennie yelled to McGregor. "It looks too clean, like I haven't been in a battle at all."

McGregor nodded to the crewmember, who smeared more mud onto the dress. Rennie shredded the hem of her skirt and ripped her sleeve.

Another yell echoed: "One minute!"

Someone handed Rennie a sword.

The set grew quiet. The lights were shut off. Only the moonlight shone down, lighting up the creek and Rennie standing on the rock. Nora was entranced. At that moment, a figure came running into the clearing.

"I need your help!" the person yelled. "I think two girls are lost out here!"

Someone shone a spotlight into the clearing. The figure stopped and covered his eyes with his hands.

"Who is that?" McGregor bellowed.

The figure dropped his arm from his face and squinted into the light. It was Luca.

CHAPTER
14

Nora got up and ran to him.

"We're okay," she yelled. "Livi and I are both okay."

"I got your text and went looking for you," said Luca as she came up next to him.

"I can't believe it went through," Nora said. "Livi's phone died hours ago."

"Yeah, I just got it," said Luca. "I was on my way to meet Carlos and see if they were still filming down here." He stopped and looked around at all the people and bright lights. "Apparently they are."

"Apparently," said Nora, smiling.

She led Luca over to Livi and Sadie.

"This is Luca," Nora told Sadie, but there wasn't time for introductions. McGregor was yelling through his megaphone again.

"I'm going to get Rennie," Sadie interrupted. "She's the only one who can keep him from freaking out."

They watched as Sadie ran over to Rennie. Meanwhile, McGregor had climbed down from his perch and was marching with two security guards across the set. The two women tried to cut him off.

"So," said Luca, looking at Nora and then Livi. "You guys found the set."

"After a few more disasters," said Livi.

Luca looked worried. "So what all happened?"

"What didn't happen?" replied Livi. "Killer bees. A car accident. A near-drowning."

"A movie director who wants to kill all of us," Nora added.

McGregor was just a few feet away. His face was even redder than before, but Rennie was trying to steer him back to his camera.

"We don't have time for this," Rennie was

saying. "Do you see the sky? The moon is setting! Stay focused."

McGregor ran his hands across his bald, sweaty head. "Just get these kids off the set," he snapped. "Put them in the tent. No one watches!"

Rennie looked at Nora. "You want to go to film school, right?" she said.

Nora nodded.

"Well, you are getting a real peek into the good, the bad, and the ugly of filmmaking." She turned back to McGregor. "They can watch, Cameron. Remember, this is my movie too."

The director looked flustered. "They can't see the ending, Rennie," he said, sounding desperate. "They could leak it to the world. It would ruin everything."

"They're not going to breathe a word to anyone about this movie," said Rennie. "Are you?" She gave them a firm look.

"No!" Nora, Livi, and Luca said at once.

"They'll sign a confidentiality agreement just like everyone else," said Rennie. She looked at Sadie, who ran off to get the forms.

They waited in uncomfortable silence. Nora knew she shouldn't say anything, but she couldn't stop herself.

"Mr. McGregor?" she said.

He glared at her. "What?" he said. "What now?"

"I was just wondering," Nora began. "Why do you film from so high up? It seems so distant." She could see his jaw tightening as she spoke, but she went on. "What if you shot from the ground? You could direct the camera up at Rennie while she's up on that rock. Then the sky and moon would be behind her. It would highlight her struggle against evil."

"You . . ." The hot color was coming back to McGregor's face. "*You* have the nerve to tell *me* how to film? Who are you to say anything?"

Nora took a step back and nearly ran into Sadie, who had appeared with a clipboard and forms in her hand.

"I was just . . ." Nora began, but Rennie interrupted.

"That would really add some depth," said Rennie, looking at Nora. "I like that idea."

They all looked at McGregor. In amazement, they watched him close his eyes and take a deep breath. He didn't yell. He didn't say anything. When he opened his eyes, he didn't look at any of them. He just headed back to his director's perch and shouted for everyone to take their places.

* * *

"Did we just sign our lives away?" Livi whispered to Sadie.

Sadie laughed. "Just your souls," she said.

"We're the living dead!" Nora said excitedly.

"Quiet on the set," someone yelled.

Everything went dark and quiet again. Only the sound of the river floated over the set.

Rennie stood strong atop the boulder. Her face was fierce. The moonlight shone down on her, casting her face in light and shadow.

McGregor angled his camera from his perch up above.

Rennie raised her sword. The light of the moon reflected off the polished silver.

On each side of the river, the vampires emerged. Nora saw the storekeeper step from behind a tree. His thin strands of black hair were stark against his white head. The moonlight made the vampires' skin look like stone.

Sword lifted, Rennie leapt off the rock and onto the riverbank. It was clear she did her own stunts, and Nora was impressed. Rennie swung the sword above her head and went after the vampires who surrounded her.

She moved to a place near the river, where a young girl in a white dress was lying still. "That's her daughter," Nora whispered to Livi. Rennie knelt down over the girl's body, shoulders shaking. She let out one of the most heartbreaking cries Nora had ever heard.

"Cut," McGregor yelled from above. "One more shot."

The girl Rennie was kneeling over sat up. A makeup artist ran over, brushed out the girl's long hair, and added more blood to her costume.

McGregor yelled more directions left and right. Someone handed him a pair of green fishing waders. He quickly put them on, grabbed a camera from one of the crew, and waded into the cold water. Rennie took her place back on the rock.

"Let's do this!" McGregor shouted. "Action!"

Nora watched as McGregor knelt in the water and began to film. He shot the scene looking up at Rennie as she stood on the rock. This time Nora felt a shiver run through her. The moon was full and bright behind Rennie, just like she'd imagined.

Rennie moved through the scene again. Her howl was even more powerful than before.

CHAPTER
15

They filmed a fight scene next. The shopkeeper's character was killed, but not before he let out a menacing laugh. The moonlight shone down and lit up his long, bony hands. Nora knew this scene wouldn't end up on the cutting room floor. It was terrifying.

More and more vampires emerged from the woods. McGregor filmed them stepping out of the shadows and into the waning moonlight. He shot them each from different angles. He shot them again and again.

Meanwhile, the sky started to turn periwinkle blue, then pink.

"One more shot!" McGregor bellowed.

The darkness was fading fast. "This isn't in the script. We're going full improv!"

He went over to Rennie and spoke to her. She nodded. Then he gathered all the surviving vampires around and said something to them. They all stood in the clearing surrounding Rennie. McGregor, practically skipping, ran back to get his camera.

"Action!" he cried.

Rennie picked up her daughter's body as the sky turned golden above her. The vampires covered their eyes as light streamed through the trees. Hissing, they retreated into the darkness of the woods. All but one. An old woman with long silver hair remained next to Rennie.

"Save her!" Rennie screamed.

The woman bent over the girl, still cradled in Rennie's arms, and bit down on her neck. Sunlight lit up the scene.

There was complete silence as McGregor filmed. Everything and everyone seemed to freeze in place.

"Cut!" McGregor shouted. "That's a wrap!"

He was smiling now, and raised his camera into the air.

Nora looked over at Livi, who had tears in her eyes. "Wow," said Livi. "You should totally do this."

Nora had a big grin on her face.

"I just want this to be my life," she said, turning to Sadie. "This. All of this. It's amazing."

"It sure is," said Sadie, nodding.

McGregor had found a ladder to stand up on. He began to speak, and cast and crew gathered around to listen.

"Thank you, everyone. Thank you," he began. He nodded to Rennie and all the vampire actors who had come from the woods. Then he looked around at his crew. "Thank you for all your hard work and dedication to this movie. You gave it everything. That was the last scene and I couldn't be prouder." He paused, looking thoughtful. "Finally, thank you, Rennie, for being my co-director. I couldn't have done it without you."

Everyone turned to Rennie and clapped again, including Livi and Nora.

"She helped direct the sequel!" Nora said.

The four of them watched the cast and crew break apart into happy, chattering groups. After thanking and hugging everyone, Rennie walked over to them.

"You were incredible," Luca and Nora said at the same time, and then looked at each other, embarrassed.

"Thank you," said Rennie. She turned to Nora and smiled. "Did you notice that Cameron took your advice?"

"I did," said Nora, beaming back. She only wished that she had been the one holding the camera.

McGregor himself headed over, holding a small black case. For the first time that night, he didn't look angry.

"Bravo," he said to Rennie. Then he looked at Nora, extended his hand, and actually smiled.

In shock, Nora reached out hers, and he shook it.

"Thank you," he said. "I think there's a very good chance you'll see your shot in this movie. I wish you luck at film school."

Nora felt her stomach fall.

"That means the world to me," she said. "But my camera and footage went into the river with our car. There's no way I'll get in without a film."

McGregor handed her the black case. "I want to give you this," he said. "It's one of the first cameras I ever shot on. There's nothing fancy about it, and it's not worth much, but it remains a favorite of mine. Maybe you can capture something amazing." Next he turned and looked at Livi. "My apologies for being such a tyrant," he added.

"Mr. McGregor, I can't accept this," said Nora. "Knowing my scene might be in the movie is more than enough."

"I'll give you a piece of advice," he replied. "Accept help when it's offered. I had a mentor, too, you know." With that, he gave a bow and walked off, the rising sun shining on his head.

"It's good advice," said Rennie with a wink. "Good luck, you three. I'm glad you're all right. And who knows—maybe we'll meet again someday." She gave them a final smile, and went to follow McGregor.

For a moment they stood in silence, in awe at her, McGregor—everything.

Then Nora looked at Livi. "Does anyone know what time it is?" she said.

Sadie checked a watch on her wrist. "About six," she said.

"Livi has an interview at Manford University at ten," Nora said. "Is anyone headed that direction?

"It's okay, Nora. We'll never make it," said Livi. "Plus, look at me. I'm half-drowned and dressed like a gym teacher. I'll call and reschedule."

Sadie shook her head. "It's important that you show up if you said you're going to be there. Trust me." She looked off for a moment, remembering something.

"My Jeep is parked a ways off," said Luca. "We'd have to get to it, but then I can drive you."

"It's a three-hour drive," said Livi. "If you speed the whole way, we'll still be late."

"No, we can make it," Sadie said, suddenly focused again. "I'm headed to San Francisco myself. Here's the plan: we'll get you cleaned up, find some decent clothes in wardrobe, and leave as soon as you're ready."

"Sadie—" Livi began.

"No, McGregor's right," Sadie said. "Everyone needs help from time to time. And I feel for you. It wasn't so long ago I needed favors from everyone I met."

Luca stood awkwardly off to the side. "Well, I guess this is good-bye, then," he said. "I'm just really glad you're both okay."

"Come with us," said Sadie. "I'll at least drive you back to your car."

"And it won't be good-bye for real," Nora said, looking at him. "I mean, if Livi ends up going to Manford, I'll have plenty of reasons to visit."

Luca grinned. "In that case," he said, "I should get Carlos to text me some of the questions they asked him. I can quiz you on the way back to my car."

"That would be great," said Livi.

"Okay, let's be quick," Sadie said, looking at Livi. "We need to make you look less like a gym teacher and more like a potential college student. Come with me."

CHAPTER
16

After getting Livi cleaned up, Sadie and Nora stood back and admired their work.

"You look great!" said Nora. "No one would believe you were attacked by bees less than twenty-four hours ago."

"Attacked by bees?" asked Sadie. "Wow. Someone should make a movie about you two."

Nora took Livi's blue sweater off the chair where they had hung it to dry. It was still caked with mud and leaves. Nora scraped off a bit of mud with her thumb.

"Your lucky sweater," she said, handing it to Livi.

Livi slid her hand into the pocket and

pulled out her phone. Not only was the battery dead, but it was also full of water.

"We still need to call Mom," said Livi. "And Mia. I'm sure they're both panicking about what happened to us."

"Use this," said Sadie, throwing Livi her phone.

"Let them both know we're fine," said Nora. "But let's wait to explain everything until *after* your interview."

"Agreed." They exchanged a look. Telling their mother what had really happened would take a long, long time.

Luca met them outside.

"All right, let's get going," said Sadie. "I know I don't have to tell you, but we're on a tight schedule!"

In the rising daylight, the three of them followed her down a path and out of the woods.

Sadie drove fast. They wove down the bumpy
mountain road and made it onto the interstate
as the sun was climbing above the trees. Once
he was home, Luca called Sadie's phone and
quizzed Livi during their drive. In no time at
all they saw the Golden Gate Bridge standing
out in the bay. And not long after that they
were rounding the turn onto Manford's
campus.

"All right, good luck!" said Luca, and
Livi hung up their call. The clock on Sadie's
dashboard read 9:37 a.m. Livi texted Mia
and then dialed their mom's phone number,
keeping her eye on the clock.

Their mother picked up, sounding panicked. Livi explained that she was on her way to her interview, that she couldn't talk, and that she'd call back in an hour.

"Did she suspect anything?" Nora asked when Livi had hung up.

"Shockingly, no," said Livi. "But she was mad we didn't call last night."

"Well, she'll be really mad when we tell her the car went into a river," said Nora.

"I think we should work on our story," said Livi. "There are some things poor Mom never needs to know."

"It will be like the scripts you used to write," said Nora.

"Exactly," said Livi.

Sadie looked at the two of them and laughed. "So you two have been in the movie business before," she said.

"A neighborhood production," said Nora, smiling. "Do you feel ready, Liv? Do you need more practice?"

"What obstacles have you overcome?" joked Sadie, and they all laughed.

"Just tell them everything that happened to you on the way to this interview," said Nora. "It's the perfect story of perseverance, determination, and grit."

"Thanks to my sister," said Livi. "I have quite the story to tell."

"Maybe we should've left some mud on your face," said Sadie.

"And some leaves in your hair for dramatic flair," added Nora.

Livi shook her head. She reached for her still-damp, mud-covered sweater. "What would really sell it is if I put this on," she said, holding up the sweater.

Sadie pulled up to a limestone building and stopped by the curb. A sign out front read *Admissions*.

"Good luck," they both told Livi as she got out.

"Just be yourself," said Sadie.

Nora added, "But don't forget to tell them about the killer bees."

They watched as Livi walked toward the building.

"Hold on," Nora shouted out the window. "Don't you want this?" She held out the sweater for Livi to see. Livi came running back to the car.

"I know something luckier," said Livi. She opened the car door and gave Nora a huge hug.

"You've got this," Nora whispered in her ear. "If you can survive a road trip with me, you can survive anything."

Livi laughed, broke free, and turned to walk into the building. A man in a blue blazer greeted her and led her inside.

Nora watched her sister disappear into the building. She had that bittersweet feeling again.

"Breakfast?" said Sadie. They headed to a café on campus to wait for Livi.

"If I had any money, I'd say breakfast was on me," said Nora. "But my wallet is also underwater."

"Breakfast is on McGregor," said Sadie. "He insisted I get you all a meal and whatever you need."

They ordered and sat at a booth near a window. While they waited for their coffee,

Sadie cleared her throat and looked at Nora.

"So you want to go to film school?" she asked.

"I do," said Nora.

"It's probably a good idea," said Sadie. "But what if you waited a year?"

"What do you mean?" asked Nora.

"What would you think about taking a gap year? You could come and intern for Rennie," said Sadie. "She was really impressed with your passion, and she's been thinking about mentoring someone."

Nora looked at her in disbelief. "Are you serious?"

"I am," said Sadie. "Think about it. You would learn things you'd never learn in a lecture hall."

"Well, I—that would be incredible."

"You can still go to school eventually," said Sadie. "But I think this internship would put you ahead of the curve. There's nothing like learning by doing."

"Yes!" cried Nora. "When would I start?"

"We start production on a new movie late

in October, but Rennie's office is down in LA. When we aren't on set, you'd be working there."

"Thank you," said Nora. "Thank you. I can't believe it."

Their coffee and food arrived, but Nora couldn't eat a thing. She was filled with excitement and disbelief. She thought about calling her mom, or Luca. But she didn't want to say anything until she told Livi first.

ABOUT THE AUTHOR

K.R. Coleman is a writer, teacher, and parent of two boys. She has written over half a dozen books for the Darby Creek Series. Some of her favorites are: *Deadman Anchor*, *Showdown*, *Truth or Dare*, and *The Freshman*. Under her real name, Karlyn Coleman, she has published short stories and a picture book entitled, *Where Are All the Minnesotans?* Currently, she is working on a young adult novel entitled, *Whispering Through the Tree Tops*.

ROAD
TRIP

HEAT WAVE

OFF COURSE

SPINNING OUT

STRANDED

DAY OF DISASTER

Would you survive?